ALPHAS
& Aces
COLORING BOOK
NEW YORK TIMES BESTSELLING AUTHOR
Susan Stoker
StokerAces.com

Alphas & Aces Coloring Book

Copyright © 2018 by Susan Stoker

Twitter: www.twitter.com/susan_stoker

Facebook (author): www.facebook.com/authorsstoker

www.facebook.com/authorsusanstoker

Goodreads: www.goodreads.com/SusanStoker

Website: www.StokerAces.com

Cover and Pages by: Jessica Hildreth at Jessica Hildreth Designs

Designer of logos: Chris Mackey of Aura Design Group

Printed in U.S.A

OPERATION
Alpha

SEAL OF PROTECTION
PROTECTING
Caroline

SEAL OF PROTECTION
PROTECTING
Alabama
SHUT UP

SEAL OF PROTECTION
PROTECTING
Fiona

SEAL OF PROTECTION
BIG BEAR LAKE CABINS
Motel
PROTECTING
Summer
Symphony No.25
1st Movement
Wolfgang Amadeus Mozart
(1756-1791)
Wolfgang Amadeus Mozart
(1756-1791)

SEAL OF PROTECTION
911
PROTECTING
Cheyenne

SEAL OF PROTECTION
ACES BAR & GRILL
PROTECTING
Jessyka

SEAL OF PROTECTION
PROTECTING
Melody

SEAL OF PROTECTION
EARTHLINGS WELCOME
LITTLE ÁLÉINN
PROTECTING
Dakota
NE
E
SE
S
SW
W
NW
N
AREA 51
TOP SECRET RESEARCH FACILITY
NO TRESPASS
VIOLATORS WILL
WITHOUT A TR

DELTA FORCE HEROES
QUIET PROFESSIONALISM RULES THE DAY.
RESCUING
Rayne
TAXI

DELTA FORCE HEROES
C2000
2-6-4-3-7
1 2 3
6 0
ON PROG STAR ENTER
RESCUING
Emily

DELTA FORCE HEROES
RESCUING
THIS IS WAR
Harley

DELTA FORCE HEROES
RESCUING
Rassie

DELTA FORCE HEROES
RESCUING
Bryn

DELTA FORCE HEROES
RESCUING
Casey

DELTA FORCE HEROES
RESCUING
Wendy
Chocolate

DELTA FORCE HEROES
BANK
RESCUING
Mary

BADGE OF HONOR
TEXAS HEROES
RIP
RIP
JUSTICE FOR MACKENZIE
TEXAS RANGER
POLICE

BADGE OF HONOR
TEXAS HEROES
Loyalty to One
JUSTICE FOR MICKIE
FEDERAL BUREAU OF INVESTIGATION
U S
DEPARTMENT OF JUSTICE

BADGE OF HONOR
TEXAS HEROES
JUSTICE FOR CORRIE

BADGE OF HONOR
HONOR
TEXAS HEROES
JUSTICE FOR RAINE

BADGE OF HONOR
TEXAS HEROES
SHELTER FOR
ELIZABETH

BADGE OF HONOR
TEXAS HEROES
HATCHER FARMS
JUSTICE FOR BOONE
BEXAR
SHERIFF
COUNTY

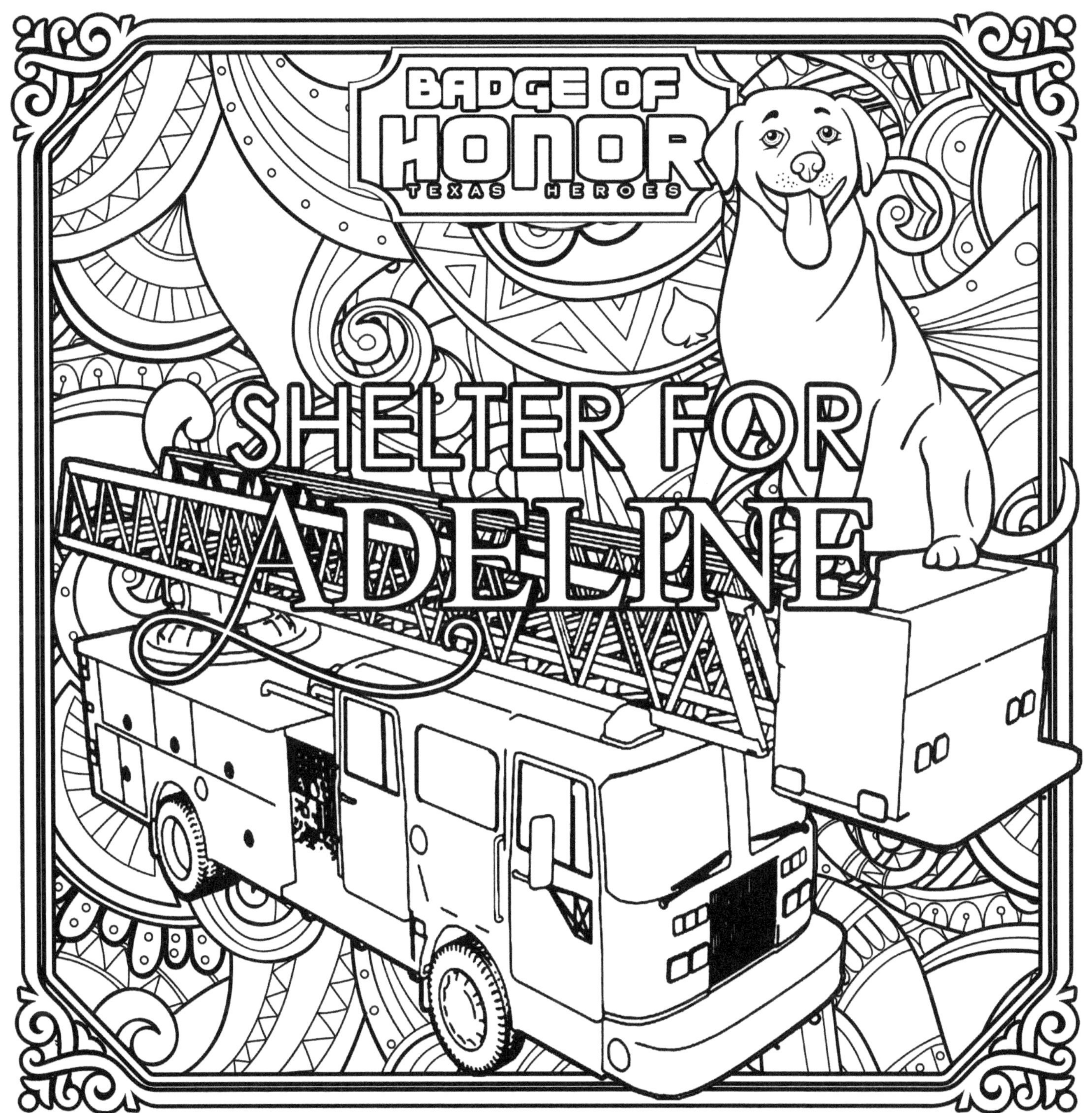

BADGE OF HONOR
HONOR
TEXAS HEROES
SHELTER FOR
ADELINE

BADGE OF HONOR
TEXAS HEROES
SHELTER FOR SOPHIE
AYÓÓ ÁNIÍNÍSHNÍ

BADGE OF HONOR
TEXAS HEROES
JUSTICE FOR ERIN

BADGE OF HONOR
TEXAS HEROES
JUSTICE FOR MILENA
HIGHWAY PATROL
U.S. ARMY

BADGE OF HONOR
TEXAS HEROES
SHELTER FOR BLYTHE

DINER
BADGE OF HONOR
HONOR
TEXAS HEROES
JUSTICE FOR
HOPE
LOTTO
Lottery
11 13 24 32 40 41
3210 2345342 32487
11 13 24 32 40 41
LOTTO
11 13 24 32 40 41
11 13 24 32 40 41

ACE
SECURITY
CLAIMING GRACE

ACE
SECURITY
CLEAR CREEK CANYON PARK
CLAIMING ALEXIS
TACOS

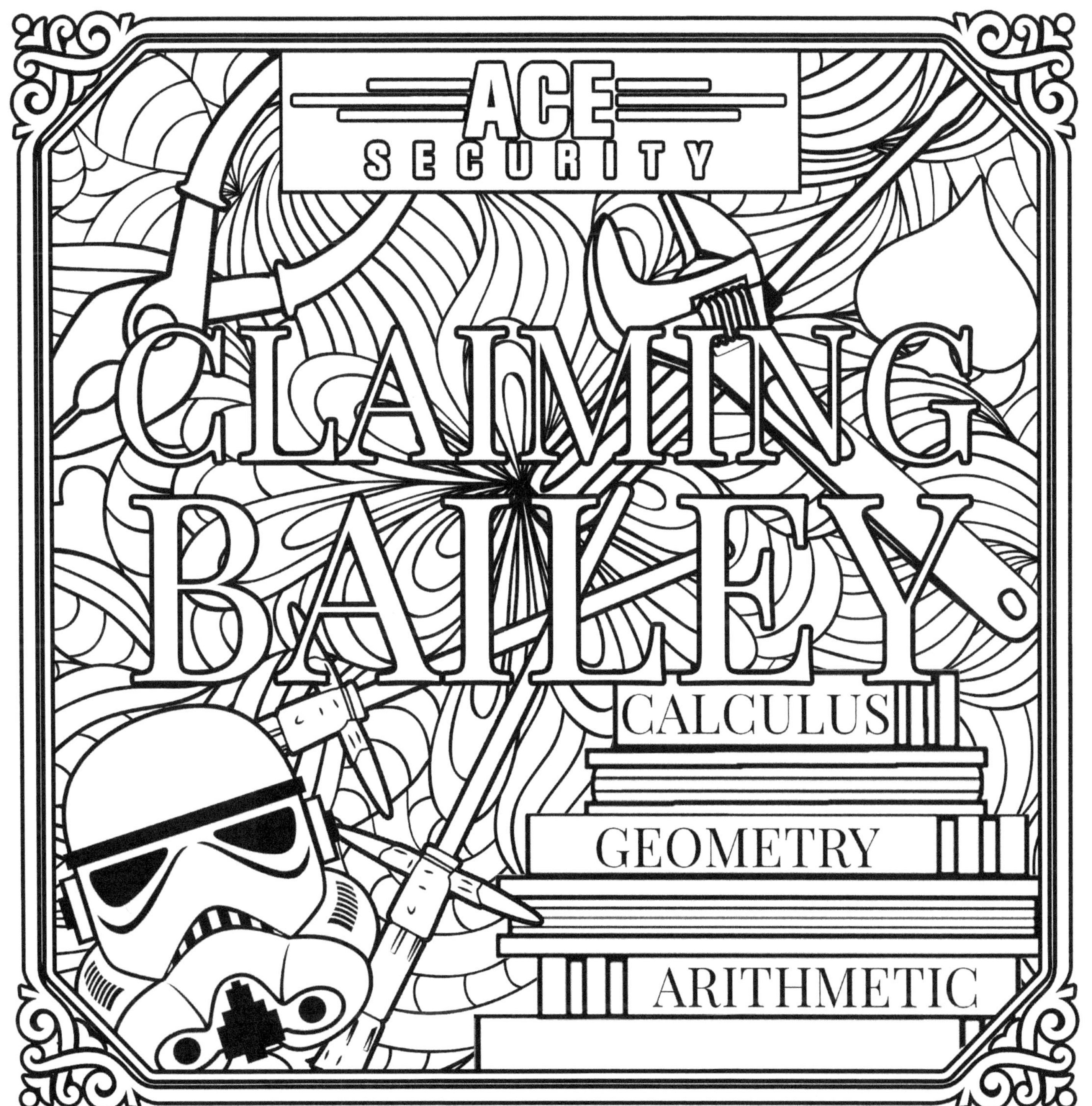
ACE
SECURITY
CLAIMING BAILEY
CALCULUS
GEOMETRY
ARITHMETIC

ACE SECURITY
CHICAGO
CLAIMING FELICITY
ROCK HARD GYM

MOUNTAIN MERCENARIES
DEFENDING ALLYE

MOUNTAIN MERCENARIES
If you love something, set it free.
DEFENDING CHLOE
8
THE PIT

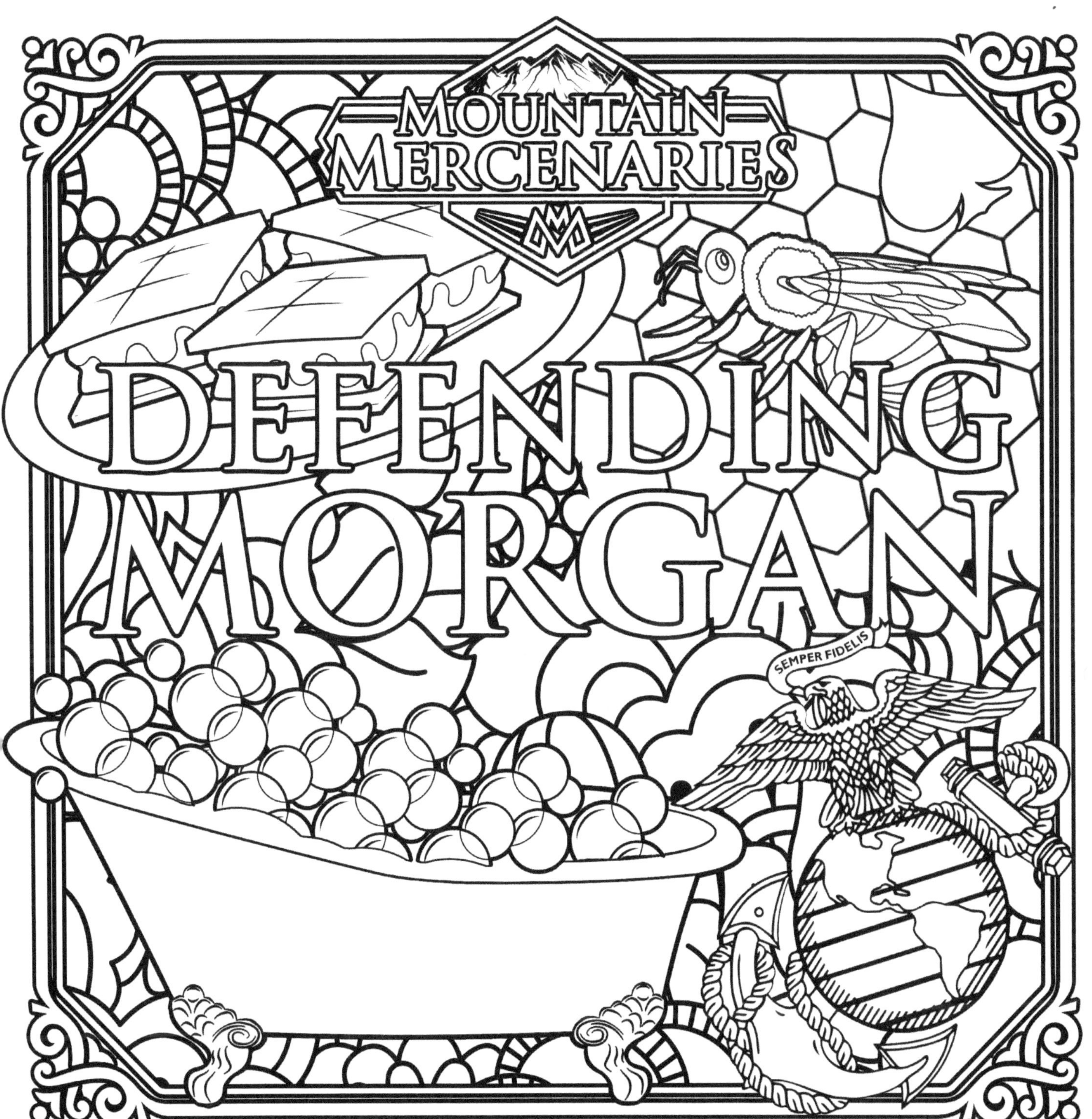
MOUNTAIN
MERCENARIES
DEFENDING MORGAN
SEMPER FIDELIS

MOUNTAIN
MERCENARIES
DEFENDING HARLOW
TOPEKA HIGH SCHOOL YEARBOOK

SEAL OF PROTECTION
LEGACY
Securing Caite
BAHRAIN

SEAL OF PROTECTION
LEGACY
Securing
SIDNEY

WHEN YOU READ A
Susan Stoker
BOOK YOU KNOW EXACTLY WHAT YOU'RE GOING TO GET.